1/07

LC 12/2/09

DreamWorks & Aardman

Flushed Away™

Movie Novel

by Penny Worms

SCHOLASTIC INC.

New York   Toronto   London   Auckland   Sydney
Mexico City   New Delhi   Hong Kong   Buenos Aires

No part of this publication may be reproduced in whole or part, stored in a retrieval system, or transmitted in any form or by any means, electronic, mechanical, photocopying, recording, or otherwise, without written permission of the publisher. For information regarding permission, write to Scholastic Inc., Attention: Permissions Department, 557 Broadway, New York, NY 10012.

Flushed Away © DreamWorks Animation L.L.C. and Aardman Animations Ltd. Flushed Away™ DreamWorks Animation L.L.C.

Published by Scholastic Inc.
SCHOLASTIC and associated logos are trademarks and/or registered trademarks of Scholastic Inc.

ISBN-13: 978-0-439-90078-2
ISBN-10: 0-439-90078-6

Designed by Rick DeMonico
Printed in the U.S.A.
First printing, November 2006

ONE

Up top, in the human world, a new day was dawning. In a smart apartment on a posh street in Kensington, a grandfather clock chimed, alerting a family that it was time to leave.

"It's nine o'clock already," said Dad. "Hurry up. We're going to miss our flight!"

"Tabitha," called Mum to her daughter. "Did you feed Roddy?"

"Uh, oh!" said Tabitha. She ran to her room and looked into the most luxurious pet cage that money could buy. Inside were all manner of toys and satin cushions. It was a palace for a pampered pet.

"Roddy?" Tabitha whispered, as she dumped a handful of food into the food bowl. "Where are you?"

Roddy, her pet rat, poked his nose out of the house. He'd been asleep but knew it was polite to respond when spoken to.

"Come on Tabitha," Dad called from down the hallway. "We don't want to miss our holiday!"

"Gotta go, Roddy!" She quickly handed him a food pellet and then ran out of the room. A moment later the front door slammed and then there was silence.

Roddy emerged from his bed and stood up. He was clearly no ordinary rat. He was wearing a mono-grammed robe and slippers.

"When the cat's away," Roddy said cheerfully, "the mice will play!"

He slid down his slide and leapt off the end, land-ing on two feet with style. Then he kicked up a food pellet and fired it from a rubber band towards the stereo. It was a direct hit and music filled the apart-ment. Now Roddy St James of Kensington was ready for his day.

He began with some morning exercise on his wheel. It was the way Roddy always started his day. He was in good shape and was proud of his appear-ance. He liked to look top notch. After his run, he grabbed his "To Do" list and expertly kicked open his cage. He had the whole huge apartment to himself and he was going to make the most of it.

First, he needed something to wear. He opted for a smart suit from his wardrobe and admired himself in the mirror. *Gosh,* he thought to himself, *how handsome am I!* Now he was ready to face his public.

His first stop was to the doll's house for a cup of tea. Roddy turned on the charm for the three dolls who lived there. They sat at the table smiling and looking beautiful, listening attentively to Roddy chatting away.

"Oh dear," said Roddy suddenly, looking at his watch. "Must fly! Thanks for the tea."

He hopped into an electric toy sports car and zoomed off. He had a whole program of activities planned — skiing, golf, and then getting ready for his date that evening — it was with Tabitha's brand-new doll, and boy was she pretty!

Using three tubs of vanilla ice-cream as his ski slope, and frozen peas for golf balls, Roddy soon checked skiing and golf off his list.

This is the life, he thought, as he lay sunning himself on the living room rug. He had two wonderful weeks like this, full of fun, freedom, and fine food from the kitchen. All he needed to do now was pop some popcorn, get the DVD ready and press his tuxedo for his date tonight.

Later that evening on his date, the pretty doll said nothing, but Roddy enjoyed her company all the same. He dropped her back at the dollhouse afterwards, lifted her arm in a wave and drove back to his cage.

"Good night!" he called. His words echoed round the apartment, but he knew she would not respond. Dolls never did. He knew — and it sometimes pained him — that there was no one else there.

TWO

Roddy was woken from his sleep by the most monstrous sound coming from the kitchen. He thought for sure it was the plumbing, but decided it'd be best to investigate. He just needed backup — someone brave and tough. Luckily, he found an old action figure at the back of the toy cupboard. Roddy checked the soldier's batteries, grabbed a flashlight, and then set off for the kitchen in his car.

"I'm armed and ready," the soldier announced, peering round the kitchen door. Roddy was behind him pressing the button to make the soldier speak.

"Give up your weapons of mass destruction!" it ordered.

It was dark in the kitchen and Roddy couldn't see anything. The deep gurgling sound seemed to be coming from the kitchen sink. Roddy climbed up and saw that the faucet was shaking. The pressure was building up. It looked as if there was a clog and it was about to be forced out.

Suddenly there was an explosion. A fountain of green gloop shot out of the tap into the air. In the stream of liquid, there was a gloopy blob with what looked like arms and legs waving in the air.

"Wahey!" cried the gloopy blob as it landed on the kitchen counter. It began to moan.

In the dim light, Roddy couldn't see exactly what or where it was. He crept towards the noise, holding his flashlight nervously in front of him. The light fell on a large and tasty-looking chocolate cake. Two hands were poking out of the top and something was emerging from the cake like a zombie rising from the grave. Roddy's flashlight unexpectedly went off. Panicking, he struggled to get it to work again. He could just make out the zombie-like thing walking towards him. Suddenly the light came on again, and Roddy could see that the zombie-like thing was a fat, filthy, smelly rat. This was Sid.

Sid let out a long, loud burp. It's strength and stench blew Roddy completely off his feet, and he fell backwards over a plate of sausages.

"Oh hello . . ." said Sid, noticing Roddy as he

was scrambling to get up. Sid licked his chocolate-covered lips. "They do *not*, repeat *not*, have food like this in the sewer." Sid was surrounded by food and it was as if he'd landed in heaven.

Roddy was appalled. "A sewer rat!" He'd never come across a sewer rat before but he'd heard that they were filthy, disease-ridden creatures, and this one certainly lacked class and manners, not to mention fashion sense.

"How did *you* get here?" Roddy asked.

"I don't know," said Sid. "One minute I'm in the pub, minding my own business, next thing you know, off I go shooting up the pipes."

Sid popped a sardine into his mouth.

"Have you got a TV?"

Roddy was taken aback. "Well yes," he stuttered, "but . . ."

"Say no more," said Sid as he bounded off the counter with a couple of sausages under his arms. He was headed towards the living room.

Roddy was aghast. What on earth was he going to do about a filthy sewer rat in the apartment? *He was going to mess up everything!* Roddy started to hyperventilate. He grabbed a brown paper bag and breathed into it slowly to calm himself down. Then he scrambled down from the kitchen counter and followed Sid into the living room.

"Wow!" cried Sid, when he first saw the television. "Look at the size of that monster!" Sid was standing in front a TV the size of a cinema screen. This place *was* heaven! He grabbed the remote control and turned on the TV.

"It's the match of the century. The World Cup final. England, Germany. Live, this Saturday. Be there!" the voice from the TV was saying.

"This place is great! I'm staying here forever!" said Sid, making himself comfortable on the sofa. He had food. He had soccer. What else could he need?

Suddenly the screen went black. Sid looked down from the sofa and Roddy was dancing around him with his fists in the air, ready to fight.

"Right, my friend," said Roddy. "You don't belong here. I'm afraid it's time for you to leave." He punched Sid's foot but immediately recoiled. Sid's feet were revolting!

"I would not do that if I were you, pal," warned Sid. "This place is mine now. I say 'jump', you say 'how high?' *Comprende*?"

Roddy couldn't believe this chap. There he was sitting on Roddy's sofa, watching Roddy's TV.

"Now fetch me some snacks from the kitchen, Jeeves. Oh, and be snappy about it," Sid demanded, really getting into the swing of things.

Sid looked Roddy up and down and raised his eyebrow. Roddy was still wearing his tuxedo, and yes, in truth he did look like a butler.

Roddy stared back at Sid. He was suddenly struck with the most brilliant plan, and for it to work he needed Sid to believe he really was his butler.

He gave a little bow. "Right away, sir," he said, getting into the role. He turned and began to walk towards the kitchen. Then he stopped and looked back at Sid, as if he'd just had a thought. "But before breakfast is served," Roddy said in a butler-like way. "Perhaps sir would like to take a dip in the hot tub?"

Sid's ears pricked up. "A hot tub?" This place was paradise!

THREE

Roddy and Sid were standing on the seat of the toilet. Roddy's plan was based on the hope that a sewer rat wouldn't know a hot tub if he was sitting in one. And it looked as if his plan was working.

"Well, after a hard day of navigating the sewer pipes," crooned Roddy, "there's nothing better than relaxing in a hot tub whirlpool bath."

Sid looked down into the toilet water. It looked so clean and fresh compared to the water he was used to down in the sewers.

"That looks so inviting," he said.

"Yes, yes, the water looks perfect. Now you hop in and I'll press this lever to get the bubbles going," Roddy said, pointing to the toilet flush. Everything was going according to plan. Soon this smelly sewer rat would be back where he belonged — in a smelly sewer!

"Right. In I go," said Sid, preparing to jump, but he stopped. "Ooh, wait, wait."

"What?" said Roddy, panic creeping into his voice.

"I know we got off on the wrong foot before, right, but you know, I really think we're going to get along. Don't you?"

"Swimmingly," Roddy laughed nervously.

Sid placed a hand on Roddy's shoulder. A moment of uncertainty passed between them. Sid looked at Roddy with pity — what a fool he was, thinking a sewer rat wouldn't know a toilet when he saw one. Roddy was worried — had he misjudged Sid?

His question was soon answered.

"Be seeing you my friend," said Sid, and he pushed Roddy into the toilet.

"NO!" shrieked Roddy. "Have mercy! I can't swim!"

"Hold your nose!" called Sid as he pulled on the handle, and Roddy St. James of Kensington was flushed unceremoniously down his own toilet.

*   *   *

As Roddy was sucked down the pipes, it was like shooting down a gigantic waterslide — only it got dirtier and murkier the further he fell. There were things floating in the water and he didn't even want to *imagine* what they were.

Just as he thought he'd never stop falling, he was spewed out of a pipe into a dark and dingy tunnel. He stood up and looked about him fearfully. The tunnel was oozing grime but at least he wasn't going to drown. He began to crawl up onto a dry ledge when he saw a small slug staring right at him.

"AAAAHHH!" shouted Roddy.

"AAAAAAHHHHHH!" shouted the slug.

They were both frozen by their fear. But it was the slug who slithered away first.

Roddy looked around him. "This is all a bad dream," he said to himself. "I'm going to open my eyes and be home." He opened his eyes, but nothing had changed. "I want to go home!" he wailed, like a snivelling rat. He struggled to get a grip of his fear. Stiff upper lip and all that. "You can get yourself out of here and you will," he said to himself. "Never forget the blood of the courageous St. James clan flows through your veins." Roddy turned to see dozens of slug eyes staring at him.

"AAAAHHH!" yelled the not-so-courageous Roddy St. James.

"AAAAAAAAAARGH!" yelled the frightened slugs.

But this time it was Roddy who ran away first. He disappeared around a corner but immediately came to a dead end. The tunnel was blocked by a metal hatch, behind which he could see light and hear a rumble of noise. Could this be a way out? Roddy pushed his way through to find out.

FOUR

Roddy landed on the pavement with a thud and looked around.

"What is this place?" he whispered to himself in awe of his surroundings. He was in a bustling city populated entirely by rats. It looked just like Picadilly Circus in the city of London up top. There were street vendors, artists, even a fountain and a ride made out of actual teacups.

"It's a real city!" Roddy exclaimed, stumbling backwards into a rat that was standing in front of the sewer floodgates.

"It's coming," the rat was saying to anyone who would listen. "The Great Flood. Those floodgates won't hold forever you know. We're doomed!"

Roddy backed away from the rat's crazy talk and

bumped into a policeman. At last! Someone who could help him.

"Oh, thank heavens," he said to the policeman. "I have got to get home, now! Up there . . . Kensington . . . the surface."

The rat policeman looked at him. "Up top? Oh, no, no, no," he said, shaking his head. "The humans don't like our sort."

"Speak for yourself," said Roddy. "They like me very much up there." But the policeman just looked at Roddy with distrust and Roddy backed away once more.

"So," came a voice next to him, "you're trying to get up top, me hardy?" It was an old burger seller flipping burgers in his van. "There's one person round here might be able to help you." He leaned forward and lowered his voice. "*Might!*" he said with caution. "Shady customer. The captain of the *Jammy Dodger*. If you can find it. . . ."

The burger seller had thrown Roddy a lifeline. Maybe the captain would help Roddy get home, and, danger or no danger, there was only one way to find out.

The burger seller took Roddy through dark and lonely tunnels to the outskirts of the city, but that was as far as the burger seller would go. Roddy had to make the final part of the journey to the *Jammy Dodger* on his own. He crept round the corner gingerly. There he saw a small boat, ingeniously made from scavenged objects. The hull was a battered iron bath, the back was a tractor tyre and the windscreen was a pair of old swimming goggles. On the boat was a sign that said NO TRESPASSING.

Roddy edged forward. "Hello?" he said, tentatively. "Er . . .permission to come aboard?" There was no response.

Roddy cautiously crept along the gangplank and stepped onto the deck. There seemed to be no one on board. He moved forward, looking around him. He didn't know it but something was behind him and following his every step — it was a large robotic hand, attached to a large mechanical arm coming from the *Jammy Dodger*'s deck. As Roddy inched forward, the hand tapped him on the shoulder and then grabbed hold of him and hoisted him high in the air. As it came level with the wheelhouse, Roddy saw someone standing in the shadows.

"Sorry," he began to say. "I didn't mean to intrude, Mr . . . Captain . . . Skipper . . . Thingy."

The figure stepped out of the shadows and to Roddy's complete surprise it was a female rat, with flaming red hair and stunning blue eyes. She was dressed in a sea-green jumper and tight Union Jack pants. She was beautiful.

"Hey," she replied. "That's Miss . . . Captain . . . Skipper . . . Thingy to you."

"Oops," said Roddy. Clearly she was a no-nonsense kind of girl.

"What are you doing on my boat?" she scoffed.

"I was told you could help me," said Roddy, and he began to tell her his hard-luck story. "You see, I've been flushed down my own toilet, half drowned, screamed at by an army of slugs . . ." His story was cut short by the thumb of the mechanical hand pressed firmly across his mouth.

Captain Rita was unsympathetic. "Yeah. Thank you. Too much information. I've got my own problems," she said.

She was suddenly distracted by the sound of an approaching boat, travelling fast and getting nearer. Rita quickly pressed a button, which released Roddy from the hand. "Stay down and keep quiet." She pulled down a tarp, which cleverly camouflaged the boat against the tunnel wall.

"Why?" asked Roddy, but Rita quickly slapped her hand over his mouth.

"I said quiet. There's rats after me who'd like to kill me," she said through gritted teeth.

"I'll contain my amazement," said Roddy, sarcastically. Rita shot him another warning glare. "Alright, alright, quiet as a mouse," whispered Roddy. But rats can rarely be as quiet as mice, especially not accident-prone rats like Roddy. He leaned back onto a rope that happened to be the boat's horn. The horn blared and suddenly the tarp dropped. Their cover was blown.

"Over there!" came a shout from the darkness.

"You idiot!" Rita snapped at Roddy.

A searchlight swung round, catching Roddy in the light. He stepped backwards, tripped over some rigging and fell overboard.

Rita heard the splash, but didn't give Roddy another thought. She pressed the button to start up the boat's engine, but nothing happened.

Coming up broadside was an enormous craft with blazing searchlights.

"Come on, *Jammy* me old mate," she pleaded. "Don't do this to me!" She desperately pressed the button again, but the engine wouldn't fire. The craft hit the *Jammy Dodger* and immediately several brutish-looking rats jumped aboard. They tried to grab Rita. She fought them with all her might, but it was no use. She was outnumbered.

One of the hench-rats fished Roddy out of the water.

"Oh, thank you, thank you," Roddy said gratefully, thinking someone had done him a favor. Then he came face to face with Whitey, a huge albino rat with fists as large as rocks. Roddy immediately shut up.

Whitey grabbed hold of both Rita and Roddy and held them in a headlock, one under each arm.

"Let me go, you pink-eyed freak!" shouted Rita, kicking and flailing. She dislodged Whitey's sunglasses from his nose.

Whitey looked at Roddy. "I'm upset now," he said in a deep, growly, cockney accent.

"Whatever's going on here, I assure you I'm not involved," Roddy pleaded.

Whitey squeezed Roddy's neck tighter.

"Ahh!" he yelled. "I'm an innocent bystander!"

Suddenly a spotlight switched on and a menacing ratty shadow appeared on the wall. Mocking laughter filled the air.

"Rita, Rita, Rita," said the shadowy figure. "You thought you could give us the slip, eh?" And with that the figure slipped all the way down the gangplank to land at Whitey's feet. Up close, he was actually a scrawny little sewer rat with spiky hair and a shrew-like nose. Spike was the type of rat that gave rats in the up-top world a bad name.

The little rat dusted down his suit and tried to regain his composure. "And who have we got here?" he said, noticing Roddy.

"I believe he said his name was Millicent Bystander," said Whitey.

Roddy was about to correct the mistake but Spike had already turned his attention to Rita.

"Where's the ruby?" he snapped at her.

"The boss wants it back," Whitey added.

Rita protested. "I don't have your stupid ruby!"

"Okay," said Spike, pacing on deck. "Are we going to do it the easy way or the hard way?"

Rita thought for a moment and then dropped her head. Looking defeated, she said slowly, "Check the tin."

"Good girl," soothed Spike. "See Whitey? This is how to do it. Watch and learn, my son. Watch and learn."

Triumphantly, Spike opened the tin of nuts but a coiled snake exploded out of it. The force of the snake propelled Spike into the air. Everyone watched as he fell back down again, landing right inside the tin, bottom first.

Rita smiled. The silly buffoon. Didn't he realise that she would *never* hand the ruby over to him? It was too valuable to her and her family.

"Was it in there?" Whitey asked Spike, revealing just how dim he really was.

Spike struggled to get out of the tin. "Right . . ." he said, flushed and angry. "Rip it up, lads!"

The hench-rats began to tear Rita's boat apart.

"Hey! Get your paws off my stuff," Rita struggled and cried as they tossed around her possessions.

Spike looked around, squinty-eyed and twitchy-nosed. "It's in here somewhere," he said. "I can feel it in me guts."

Roddy couldn't take any more. "Would you please tell these people I'm not involved in this?" he pleaded to Rita.

"Fine," she snapped. "All right. This gentleman,

he's not from around here. Just look at how nicely he's dressed." The gang all looked at Roddy. "And why?" she went on. "Because he's an international jewel thief who stole the ruby from me. If you put me down, I'll help you get it back."

Roddy was stunned. He'd liked the bit about being nicely dressed but a jewel thief! He was about to protest his innocence again but Spike spoke first, "It's time to bring out the persuader," he announced, and he pulled out a Christmas nutcracker and brandished it in front of Roddy's face.

Rita gasped. Roddy gasped. Whitey gasped, caught up in the moment.

Roddy's eyes began to water at the thought of what they would do to him. He tried to squirm his way out of Whitey's headlock. Rita seized the opportunity to make a break for it, but Whitey reeled her back in, only she was now facing the other way.

Roddy noticed something. "Look at her bottom!" he cried. There was a big bump in her Union Jack pants.

"I mean, don't you think it's rather oddly shaped?" Roddy asked.

"You little snitch!" snapped Rita.

"The booty's in the booty," said Whitey, catching

on. He lifted Rita up and shook her upside down. A ruby fell out of Rita's pants and landed on the deck. It was huge and sparkly and beautiful. All the hench-rats murmured in amazement.

"Oh, ho, ho, ho," laughed Spike. "The boss is gonna be well happy with us."

The only one who wasn't happy was Rita. And in her eyes there was only one rat to blame. Roddy was toast.

Whitey pushed Rita and Roddy through large wooden doors into a grand room. There was a real fire roaring in the hearth and someone was sitting in front of it in a throne-like armchair, listening to the radio.

"*In two short days,*" the radio announcer was saying, "*England plays Germany in the final of the World Cup. By three o'clock on Saturday, every single television set in the country will be tuned in.*"

"Boss?" Spike called. "We're back."

But the figure in the armchair didn't move.

"I got it, boss," said Spike. "The ruby. I found it."

"Well, technically, Spike," corrected Whitey, "it was Millicent who found it."

"Actually, uh, the name is Roddy," he approached the boss. "In exchange for my assistance I was hoping you might . . ."

Suddenly a long pink tongue shot out from behind the chair and snatched a fly that had been buzzing around the room.

Slightly put off, Roddy continued nonetheless, "Er . . . hoping you might help me out of the pickle I'm in."

"He *is* the pickle you're in, genius," sniped Rita.

At this, the boss stood up and turned towards them. Roddy stared in amazement. The boss was an enormous green toad wearing a purple jacket and cravat.

The Toad came towards them. "Hello, Rita," he said. "Who is this? Is your new boyfriend a waiter?"

"Boyfriend!" exclaimed Rita.

"Waiter!" exclaimed Roddy, just as appalled by the idea.

Laughing at his own joke, The Toad held out his webbed hand towards Spike. Spike dropped the ruby into it.

"The prize returns to me," The Toad said smugly. He gave it a polish on his jacket and lifted it up to the light to admire its beauty.

"That jewel belongs to my father and you know it!" protested Rita.

The Toad sneered. "Your *father*! A good for nothing scavenger just like his daughter."

Roddy tried once more to plead his case for release. Surely such a finely dressed toad would help out a fellow gentleman? But The Toad was distracted by another fly buzzing around the room. While one eye followed the fly, the other remained fixed on Rita and Roddy. Suddenly, The Toad's tongue lashed out and snatched the fly. Then both eyes once again focussed on the two other nuisances in his life — Rita and Roddy.

"Dispose of them," he ordered, and he turned away.

"No, please!" said Roddy, pitifully. "I just want to get home to Kensington!"

Without realising it, Roddy had said a magic word. The Toad's face lit up and he turned to look at Roddy. "Kensington? The Royal Borough. Up top?" he asked.

"Yes! Up top!" Roddy was nodding furiously.

"Huzzah!" said The Toad, smiling. "A man of quality!"

Roddy visibly relaxed. Finally he had met someone who understood his breeding and social standing.

"Come," beckoned The Toad. "Let me show you my private collection. I know you'll find it diverting."

The Toad led Roddy to the other side of his lair where he stopped in front of velvet curtains. Whitey pulled a rope and the curtains pulled back to reveal a treasure trove — not of glittering jewels or precious antiques, but of cheap tacky tourist objects of which The Toad was clearly very proud.

"My shrine to beauty," he announced, ushering Roddy along. "Works of high art crafted in tribute to our beloved Royal Family."

Roddy tried to disguise his amusement. How could The Toad confuse such worthless objects with high art? But he was delighted that The Toad had taken him into his confidence.

"Come," said The Toad, "let us restore the heart and highlight of my collection," and with a flourish, The Toad pulled out the ruby and placed it upon an upturned flashlight in the centre of his collection. Spike hit the switch and light beamed through the ruby while the British National Anthem played. It was a moment of sheer awe and pride to all in the room but Roddy and Rita.

Ceremony over, Roddy was anxious to turn the

conversation back to his release. "I'd love to see more of your collection," he said. "It's very amusing, but . . ."

The Toad stopped in his tracks.

"Amusing?" The Toad was frowning. All the other rats winced, knowing that Roddy had just put his posh foot in his mouth.

Rita smiled smugly — now that stuck up little fool was going to get it.

Roddy backtracked fast. "Didn't you say I'd find it amusing?" he said tentatively to The Toad.

"Diverting!" said The Toad. "Not amusing!"

"Ah," said Roddy, thinking fast. "I really meant it in the sense of the ancient Greek Muse, the goddess of inspiration . . ." As he gestured frantically, he managed to knock down, domino-style, The Toad's whole collection.

The Toad was so furious his neck began to swell.

Whitey grabbed Roddy by the shoulders and everyone knew he was done for.

"Ice him!" shouted The Toad. "Ice them both!"

#

Whitey pushed Roddy and Rita towards a large refrigerator that was glowing and humming in the corner.

The Toad signalled to Fat Tony, a large hench-rat with a small head and big ears, to open the refrigerator door.

Roddy and Rita gasped at what was inside the refrigerator — rows and rows of ice-blocks containing rats, all frozen with fear and panic on their faces.

"Former enemies, one and all," boasted The Toad. "Thieves, double-crossers, and do-gooders." The Toad cackled as a cage made out of an upside down blender was lowered around Roddy and Rita, who had been locked together with a large chain. "Prepare to meet your maker," announced The Toad. "Your ice maker!"

Whitey chuckled. "Makes me laugh every time," he said to Spike.

Two hench-rats, Ladykiller and Thimblenose, turned the valves on two tanks next to the refrigerator — one was water, the other was liquid nitrogen. Released into the blender at the same time, they would immediately freeze into a block of ice, with Rita and Roddy frozen inside, just like all the others.

Rita remained as cool as a cucumber. "There's a paper clip in my back pocket," she said to Roddy. "See if you can get it."

"Got it," said Roddy, after fishing around in her pockets.

Meanwhile standing above them, Spike began to complain of the cold as nitrogen gas began escaping from the pipes around them.

"That's why I wore me mittens," said Whitey, very pleased with his himself.

"Hit men don't wear mittens!" screeched Spike. "Take 'em off, you're embarrassin' me."

"Well it's alright for you, you've got little hands," complained Whitey.

"Well they may be small, but these are lethal weapons these," said Spike, doing a few karate chops to demonstrate.

He had no idea that underneath him, Rita had managed to pick the lock on the chains. With Roddy's help, she climbed up to the top of the blender and opened the hatch below them.

Spike and Whitey were still arguing about their hands when Rita knocked them off their feet into the blender. White gas whirled around them as the pressure levels in the tanks reached the green zone. It was icing time!

"Goodbye, vermin," said The Toad and without realising that his own hench-rats were in harm's way, he pressed a big button that said PUSH FOR ICE.

It happened in seconds. Liquid nitrogen and water poured into the blender and froze instantly, making another beautiful white-blue block of ice. The blender lifted and the mist slowly cleared.

"Now, let me see the latest addition to my . . . cubist collection," said The Toad, walking towards the block of ice and the two figures frozen inside. But they were not Roddy and Rita. They were Whitey and Spike, frozen in mid-fall. Whitey was still wearing his pink mittens.

The Toad began to swell up in anger again.

"Oi! Kermit," came a shout from above. It was

Rita, laughing and holding up her ruby. "The prize returns to me!" she said, mimicking The Toad.

Furious, The Toad smashed the ice block. "After them!" he barked at Spike and Whitey, but they were still frozen and fell to floor with a crash.

This was lucky for Rita, who hadn't yet come up with an escape plan. She looked around her and spotted a thick electrical cable that ran from outside the window down to a dock far below. Roddy looked out of the window too and immediately felt dizzy — two of his greatest fears were heights and water, and there was water underneath the cable, all the way to the dock. Rita wasn't put off in the slightest. She spotted another short cable plugged into two different sockets. She ran over and yanked it out, which caused all the lights to go off.

The Toad yelled with alarm. "Not the master cable!"

Rita ran back to the window and looped the short master cable over the thick electricity cable that ran out of the window.

"We have a plan?" Roddy asked hopefully.

Rita grabbed hold of both ends of the master cable. Roddy realised she had made a zip wire, which could take them out of the window and down to the dock.

"Wait, wait," he said urgently. "That'll never hold both of us."

"You're right," said Rita. "Toodle-oo," and she prepared to jump.

Roddy quickly weighed his options. He looked towards Spike and Whitey, now defrosted and advancing towards him. Then he looked at Rita, about to leap off a high window ledge and travel, on a wire, over a vast area of water. Roddy decided to take his chances with Rita. Just as she jumped, he leapt after her, desperately grabbing hold of her belt as she jumped out the window and zoomed down the wire.

"Let go," Rita shouted down to him. "You're too heavy."

"I can't swim!" said Roddy, clinging on to her belt for dear life. He looked down at the sea, far, far below. "I'll drown."

They were whizzing down the wire together and her belt was slowly breaking. Suddenly it snapped and they both fell, but luckily not very far. Below them was a pipe, on which Rita landed elegantly.

Roddy landed with a *smack,* face-first, but at least he was alive.

Back at the window, Spike and Whitey had watched their descent.

"Do something!" shouted Spike.

Whitey grabbed the first thing he could lay his hands on to follow Rita down the zip wire. It was Spike. He threw Spike over the electricity cable and hanging on to his head and feet, he jumped, just as Rita had done with the master cable. But the weight of the two of them on the cable dislodged the plug it was connected to from the wall and they went into free fall, plummeting towards the water.

"Keep your legs straight when you hit the water!" warned Spike to Whitey.

Whitey splashed into the water, with his legs perfectly straight as instructed. It was a clean entry and Whitey bobbed back up unhurt. His little friend had also kept his legs straight, but unfortunately there was no sea below him — he fell hard onto the dock. This was turning into a very bad day for Spike.

The same could be said for Roddy. After Rita had fashioned a new belt from the master cable, she jumped down the pipework like a gymnast, gracefully landed on the ground, and took off down an alley.

Roddy stood up on the pipe. "If she can do it . . ." and off he went — *thwack, smack, crack* — bashing into every pipe on the way down, until he finally landed with a bump on the ground.

He turned to see Whitey picking up a crumpled Spike from the dock. With one yank, Spike was straightened out and they resumed the chase. Every bone in Roddy's body ached, but he needed to get out of there. With Spike and Whitey close behind, Roddy took off down the alleyway in search of Rita. After all, she was the only person who could help him get home.

As Roddy crossed a drawbridge, he looked down and saw that the *Jammy Dodger* was about to pass underneath him. What luck! He was about to call to Rita, but suddenly the bridge started opening to allow the *Dodger* to pass underneath, and Roddy's legs were on either side of the growing divide.

Spike and Whitey had managed to catch up. "You look pretty ridiculous now, Millicent," called Spike, as Roddy's legs were stretched wider and wider.

He fell.

"Keep your legs straight," called Whitey thoughtfully. But the advice was just as useless for Roddy as it had been for Spike. Roddy crashed down onto the deck of Rita's boat. His landing jerked the boat and Rita fell forward onto the accelerator. The *Jammy Dodger* shot forward and Rita was thrown backward with such a force that the ruby flew out of her hand. She chased it around the deck of the boat as it bounced off a tennis racket, over her head, onto the canopy of the boat, and then slowly rolled down into the chain motor. The chain carried the ruby into the air and when it came back down, Rita's precious ruby disappeared down the back of Roddy's shirt collar as he struggled to get up from the deck.

"What are you?" she asked. "Some kind of bad luck boomerang? Give me back my ruby!" she yelled. She slammed into him and the ruby dislodged from Roddy's collar and was once again launched into the air.

"I haven't got your ruby!" said Roddy, holding out his empty hands. The ruby fell from the sky right into them. "Okay," he acknowledged. "*Now* I've got your ruby."

Rita tried to grab it, but Roddy pulled his hands back.

"Ah, ah, ah!" he said playfully, twirling it around in his fingers.

Rita looked worried. "Please be careful!" she said anxiously. "That ruby means a lot to me. It's priceless."

Roddy took a closer look. His expression changed. "Hold on," he said. "It's a fake." Rita started to argue. "No, look!" Roddy insisted. "It's just glass. You can tell. Watch this . . ." And with that he brought the ruby down against the boat railing and — *smash!* — it shattered into a million tiny pieces.

"There, you see," said Roddy. He was right. "You can't break a real ruby."

Rita was motionless, a look of complete horror on her face. She couldn't believe that with one swift movement, Roddy had ruined all her hopes and dreams.

Roddy saw the expression on her face. "Look on the bright side," he said, trying to put a positive spin on things. "Once The Toad knows it's worthless, he'll probably stop chasing you for it." He smiled nervously. "Roddy St. James saves the day!"

At that, Rita punched him squarely in the face.

"Good grief!" Roddy was unprepared for that. "You try to do somebody a favor . . ."

Furious, Rita picked up something, *anything,* to throw at Roddy.

"That ruby," she yelled as she fired object after object at him, "was from Queen Elizabeth's crown! It fell down the drains of Buckingham Palace! That ruby was going to change . . . my . . . life!" She loaded a makeshift bow using crayons for arrows. As the crayons rained down on Roddy, he grabbed the nearest thing to protect himself. It was a cell phone.

The crayons hit the phone's buttons and it began to ring.

"Hello?" said the voice on the phone. "May I help you?"

Roddy thought he'd been thrown a lifeline. There was someone out there who might help him. "Yes, I'm being attacked by a mad woman!" he ranted. "She's got crayons!" But suddenly he realised the missiles had stopped coming. He peeked out from behind the phone to see. Rita was slumped on the deck, her head in her hands, fighting back tears.

Roddy didn't quite know what to do. He had never had to deal with tears before. His doll friends only ever smiled. He put down the phone and went tentatively over to her.

"Rita . . ." he began, uncertain of what to say next.

"Just go away please," said Rita, strength

returning to her face and voice. She got up and walked away, not wanting Roddy, or anyone, to see her crying.

"I'm . . . sorry," said Roddy. He wasn't expecting this apology to heal the hurt, but it was the only thing he could think of to say.

Roddy was surprised at how venomously Rita turned on him. "Ha! Sorry?" she yelled. "Me and my dad worked these drains for years. He broke every bone in his body trying to get that ruby." She stopped. The thought of her father now in a wheelchair because of a worthless piece of red glass made her see how worthless it had all been. "It was going to be the answer to all our prayers, and now it turns out it was a stupid fake."

Roddy felt horrible. He stood watching her for a second, unable to move or speak for fear of making matters worse.

Then an idea came to him. It was a brilliant idea. A genius idea! An idea to solve both their problems in one go. Roddy St. James of Kensington could still save the day!

"Maybe I can make it up to you?" he said.

"Impossible," Rita responded.

"I mean it!" said Roddy. "Back at my place,

we've got a jewelery box crammed with rubies and diamonds. REAL ones! So all you have to do is get me home to Kensington and I'll make you rich beyond your wildest dreams."

Rita slowly turned to face him.

"How do I know this ain't just a load of old rubbish?"

It was a fair question, Roddy thought, so he gave her a fair response. "I suppose you're just going to have to trust me," he said, holding her gaze.

Trust? Trust this floppy-haired fool? She shook her head at the idea. Then she looked at him again. He might be an upper-class nincompoop, but maybe he did have a stash of jewels. Besides, she had no other option.

"Alright," she said, spitting into her hand. "You've got yourself a deal."

She held out her hand to Roddy, her spit dripping from her palm. Roddy had never experienced the ways of sewer rats before and he found this particular practice very distasteful, but if it was going to get him home. . . .

He leaned forward to spit into her hand too.

"Your OWN hand!" she barked.

Very delicately, Roddy dribbled into his palm.

Rita grabbed it and they shook. The deal had been struck. Roddy forced a smile, but he felt very uncomfortable with all that spit in his hand. Rita forced a smile too, but she wasn't going to let down her guard. Not for one minute.

SEVEN

The Toad was standing in front of his window looking out over the sewer. His gaze was on the floodgates that dominated the background.

"The sands of time whisper through my flippers . . ." he mused. "Where *are* those idiots?"

He turned towards a large jar next to him. It was full of smiling tadpoles wearing baby bonnets.

"Come on out my lovelies," he said to his babies in a baby-soft voice. "Cheer your old dad up. Poor Daddy, surrounded by filthy rats in this joyless, sunless void! But don't worry, little men. Daddy will get rid of them all. He'll flush them away, yes he will. They'll all be deady-weddy."

The Toad began to kiss the jar. Then he heard a wet, sloshing noise behind him. Spike and Whitey

RODDY

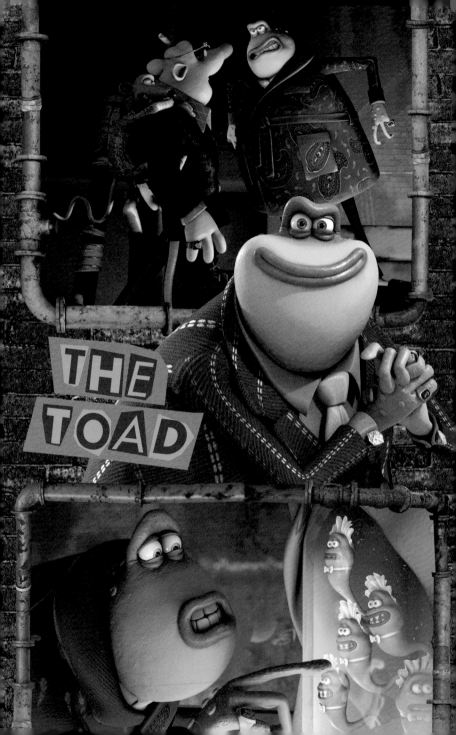

THE
TOAD

WHITEY

LE FROG

had entered the room wearing makeshift diving gear. They looked ridiculous.

The Toad quickly covered up the jar and pulled himself together. "Did you find it?" he asked hastily.

Spike and Whitey held out fragments of the ruby. They tried to make light of the situation, suggesting other ways The Toad could use the fragments — earrings, a chandelier — but The Toad knocked the glass splinters out of their hands.

"Forget the ruby!" he hollered. "It's the master cable that I want! The one that grubby creature Rita took."

It took a moment for this information to sink in to their little rat brains.

"Without it," The Toad continued to rant, "my plan is ruined!"

Desperate to please, Spike said, "Okay chief. Forget the ruby. Ruby's gone. We are now your cable guys."

"Focused," agreed Whitey. "Cable-centric, Boss."

The Toad looked at them both with contempt. It was impossible to get good help nowadays, but he was stuck with these two and they were nothing if not willing.

He spelled it out to them. "You need to be back in time for the World Cup Final."

"Oh great," said Spike enthusiastically. "Are we watching the game together, Boss?"

"No, we are not, you moron," snapped The Toad. There was clearly more to his plan than he was prepared to let on. "Just get me the cable!"

EIGHT

At that very moment, the cable in question was around Rita's waist. She was backing the *Jammy Dodger* into a rickety wooden jetty.

"One quick stop, just need to pick up some maps for the journey," said Rita as she moored the boat.

Roddy looked up at the house in front of them. It was wooden shack perched on thin stilts above the water. It looked as if it would fall apart if anyone so much as sneezed. Rita's weight on the jetty made it lean and creak.

"Is that a house?" Roddy asked. There was no way he wanted to be inside the house when it fell down.

"Actually, you know what, it is dangerous. I'll only be a minute," Rita replied, annoyed by the way he was looking at her family's home. She walked away leaving him on the jetty.

As Rita disappeared into the house, Roddy heard excited voices inside. He went over to the window to see a little hoard of red-headed children all jumping and swinging and leaping.

"Rita's home!" they squealed. As they rushed towards her, the whole house leaned to one side. Rita gave out presents galore, all gifts from the up-top world that had found their way into the sewer.

Roddy watched as Rita's mother came into the room. "Oh Rita, thank goodness you're safe," and she gave her a huge hug, a mother's hug. Roddy felt a pang of longing. This was what having a family was all about.

The house lurched again and a wheelchair rolled into the room. "Rita!" said her dad. Rita walked in to find her dad sitting in his wheelchair; both arms in casts and set wide apart as if ready to give Rita a hug. She hugged him awkwardly.

"Mum, there's a peeping tom outside," called Liam, one of Rita's brothers, spotting Roddy by the window.

"That's just my passenger," said Rita grumpily.

"He's very good looking," Rita's mother added, noticing Roddy's tuxedo.

"He's *not* coming in," Rita swore, but there was no stopping her mum and grandma. They were both quite taken with Roddy's posh appearance.

As they all sat down for soup, Rita's family got to asking questions. The women wanted to know if Roddy was Rita's boyfriend. Grandma hoped Roddy would sing a song. But Rita's father and brother Liam had other things on their mind when they heard about Rita and Roddy's plan.

"It's impossible," her father cried as he dragged Rita into the back room for a private conversation. "No one's ever got past the rapids at Hyde Park. Once the current gets you, you're sucked into the Treatment Plant and boiled alive in bleach."

"But Dad," protested Rita, "he's going to pay us." Her dad sighed. "For the last time," he said with frustration, "we don't need money." He slammed his fist down on the table. The table immediately collapsed. Then the oven door fell off and crashed through the floor, splashing into the water below. The house creaked and tilted alarmingly.

Rita tried to not look too shaken by his words as

she headed for the living room. Before she could join the others, her brother Liam asked to have a word with her.

Liam held up the WANTED poster with a picture of Roddy. It said WANTED. MILLICENT BYSTANDER.

"I've got a plan," he said quietly. "Just tell The Toad it's all his fault and get the reward instead," said Liam.

Helping to clear the dinner dishes, Roddy headed for the kitchen. Suddenly, he heard Rita's voice. "So I hand Roddy over to The Toad and claim the reward. Then we're all sitting pretty for the rest of our lives, is that the idea?"

"Yeah," Liam replied. "The Toad'll pay a fortune for him, and he's a bad one anyway, so who cares?"

Roddy couldn't believe his ears. *She was going to turn him over to The Toad!* For a moment he didn't know what to do, but then he left the house without a noise.

Rita's dad had joined the conversation and gave Liam a clip round the ear. "You cheeky little monkey. I won't have no son of mine acting the rat."

Rita joined in. "Liam, our family never goes back on our word."

Liam looked out of the window and saw Roddy

leaving on the *Jammy Dodger*. "Well perhaps you should tell him that when you catch up with him."

A look of panic crossed Rita's face. Roddy was leaving! Worse still, he was taking the *Jammy Dodger* with him. She ran down to the jetty.

"I thought we had a deal!" she hollered at Roddy as he was sailing away.

"So did I!" Roddy shouted back. He felt he owed her nothing — she was about to betray him after all.

"You conniving little . . ." Rita was shouting from the jetty. There was no way she was going to let Roddy steal the *Jammy Dodger* from her. She looked around for something on which she could follow him — and there it was, a plastic duck. It was embarrassing, but it would do.

Roddy had never skippered a boat before and it showed. The *Jammy Dodger* swerved wildly as it travelled down the narrow sewers, bumping and scraping along the tunnel walls. Suddenly the engine sputtered and cut out completely. At first Roddy felt defeated, but then a steely determination came over him. He didn't need Rita. He could do this himself. So he set about trying to fix the engine. As soon as he touched it, he yelped in pain.

"Ooh! Fairly major burn to the hand there, smell of burning flesh," he said to himself. He didn't realise, but he'd also singed his hair. In a rage, he kicked the engine and immediately regretted it.

"*Start,* you worthless old pile of rubbish," he screamed at the engine. "You . . . you useless, unreliable . . ."

"Untrustworthy, double-crossing, two-faced, conniving little toe-rag!" It was Rita and she was happy to help him finish his list of insults — only her comments were directed at Roddy not at the *Jammy Dodger*'s engine. She had caught up with him on the duck, and was she mad!

"I'm the double-crosser?" Roddy challenged, his hair still smoking. "That's rich. I overheard *every-thing*. Yes, you and your family were going to sell me to The Toad!"

This stopped Rita in her tracks. This was the last thing she expected to hear, but when she replayed the conversation with her dad and brother in her head, she realised what had happened.

"That was my stupid little brother's plan . . . and no one listens to him!" she said.

"Oh," said Roddy. "Must have missed that part."

"How could you think I'd sell you out," said

Rita. "When I make a deal, I make a deal." She fixed him with a glare, and added, "Your hair's on fire."

Roddy began to pat his head frantically.

"Look, I'm sorry alright?" said Roddy after he'd put out the fire. "I was wrong. Now I think we should just put it behind us . . . if you're big enough." Roddy calculated that someone as proud as Rita would always rise to a challenge.

"Oh, I'm big enough, Roddy," Rita said, nodding and smiling. "I can put it *right* behind me." And with that she forced Roddy overboard. She wasn't *so* heartless that she'd leave a rat unable to swim in the middle of the water. He had the rubber duck after all!

"This is such an over-reaction!" Roddy reasoned. "I mean, you can't just leave me here on a duck! Up the creek without a . . ."

Rita threw him a child's ukulele to use as a paddle.

"Fine, *fine*!" Roddy said. "I have more chance of getting out of here on this than in that old tub." He nodded towards the *Jammy Dodger*. Without an engine, it was going nowhere.

"Really," said Rita calmly.

"If it were a horse they'd shoot it . . ." said Roddy, thinking he was being witty.

The smirk was immediately wiped off his face when Rita held up a funnel and a can of fuel.

". . . which would be a shame," he said, "because it obviously just needs a little fuel." He felt like such a fool — and he looked like one, too.

Roddy was paddling frantically behind the *Jammy Dodger* as Rita began to sail away.

"Look, if you're trying to teach me a lesson, consider it taught!" shouted Roddy. "I'm on a duck, begging!" But Rita was unforgiving. She began to accelerate down the tunnel and was going to leave Roddy in her wake, but he saw a rope trailing behind the *Jammy Dodger* and grabbed hold of it.

Suddenly there was music coming from behind Rita. She turned to see that Roddy had attached one of the *Jammy Dodger*'s mooring ropes to the duck and now he was gliding along behind her. He strummed the ukulele and began to sing:

"Ice cold Rita
Never did I meet a . . .
Girl who was half so cruel.

I offered her a jewel —
But she left me stuck
Stranded on a duck
What a shoddy
Thing to do to Roddy.
Me.
That's Roddy St. James of
Kensington."

Some slugs sitting on the sewer ledge began to
join in:

"Poor, poor Roddy
Flushed down his own potty.
Rita, can't you find it in your heart
To help him?"

Roddy began to harmonize with the slugs:

"How mean can one rat be?
Ice cold Rita,
Won't you be sweeter to me?"

It was a silly song, and the slugs' harmony was
enough to melt the coldest of hearts. Suddenly the

Jammy Dodger's mechanical arm swung out and hoisted Roddy into the air above the deck.

"Am I forgiven?" Roddy asked.

"Nope," she said curtly. "I was just afraid you'd sing another verse."

Roddy looked at her. "Rita?" he said. The tone of his voice instantly changed the mood on board. "I wasn't eavesdropping," he said earnestly. "I was actually . . . just watching you with your family . . . thinking how lucky you were."

"Lucky? Stuck with you?" said Rita, but there was a hint of affection in her voice and she pushed a button, releasing the hand and dropping Roddy onto the deck.

"So our deal's still on?" asked Roddy.

"Sure it is," said Rita, and with that Roddy spat into his hand and offered it to her. Rita spat too and they shook. She had taught him to do one thing properly at least.

NINE

Rita gave Roddy the only job on board she thought he was capable of. He was sitting on a swing scraping barnacles from the side of the *Jammy Dodger*. It was from here that Roddy saw the speed-boat approaching rapidly. At the helm were Spike and Whitey.

"There they are!" yelled Spike. "Go get 'em lads."

Suddenly, from out of the side sewers, came the hench-rats — Thimblenose Ted, Ladykiller, and Fat Tony, all riding hand-blenders. They were cutting through the water at top speed.

"Rita!" Roddy yelled.

Rita whirled round, but unlike Roddy she didn't panic. She waited until Thimblenose Ted was about to make a grab for the boat and then she slammed down the throttle. The change in speed made Thimblenose almost fall off his blender.

"Hold on!" she shouted to Roddy, still on the swing. He was whipping around wildly in midair while she tried to shake off the hench-rats.

The speed of the blenders was too much for the *Jammy Dodger*. The hench-rats were getting closer and closer to Roddy's tail.

"Can we go a little faster?" Roddy yelled to Rita.

"We don't have to," she yelled back. She had a plan. "Go, go, purple custard!" And with that she pulled a lever that opened a door in the side of the Dodger. Inside the compartment was a packet of Dessert Mix. The pink powder began spewing out into water, and when Fat Tony's hand blender hit the mix, it was instant Angel Delight! He was stuck fast in a wave of sugary froth.

Roddy was impressed. But then Thimblenose Ted came screaming around the mountain of dessert. Rita looked ahead. They were heading straight towards a dock and houses! She pulled the wheel round sharply to turn the boat, which meant Roddy went flying through the air like a trapeze artist. He went smacking into Thimblenose and threw him off his blender.

Rita quickly pressed the button for the mechanical arm to pull Roddy in, but Ladykiller grabbed at his leg. Roddy needed to think fast — which hadn't been his speciality up till now — but he saw a chance.

"Rita, try and go right," he shouted to her.

"What?" *Was he nuts?*

"Just trust me," he yelled.

It wasn't easy for Rita to trust anyone, let alone a posh twit with about as much knowledge of the sewers as the Queen of England.

"I hope you know what you're doing," she yelled back and spun the wheel right.

Ahead of them was a low bridge. Just in front of it was a buoy floating in the water, attached to it by a rope was a giant inflatable lizard advertising the "LONDON SAYS 'BOAT SMART!'" campaign.

"Head for the rope," yelled Roddy to Rita.

She swerved the Dodger to the side so Roddy could grab the rope and then she steered the boat under the low bridge.

BOOMPHH! The inflatable lizard jammed under the bridge arch behind them, blocking the entrance.

Ladykiller couldn't stop his blender in time and he went careening into the lizard, bouncing back in the direction of Thimblenose Ted. There was a loud splash.

"Hooray!" shouted Roddy. "We did it!"

"Well done, Roddy!" said Rita, but they had spoken too soon. There was a *POP!* and then Spike and Whitey zoomed through the bridge in their speedboat.

Rita hastily pressed the button to get Roddy back on board.

"Thank you," he said.

"You're welcome." And with that the *Dodger* roared away.

Not to be outdone, Spike was preparing for a launch. He was standing on a coil-sprung rat trap, armed with an old-fashioned can opener. He had a telephone cord as a safety harness, and was waiting for Whitey to pull the release.

"Are you sure about this, Spike?" asked Whitey. "These things are supposed to be dangerous."

"Danger," said Spike, "is my middle name."

"I thought it was Leslie," said Whitey, not quite getting the point, but still he released the clip. Spike flew through the air and landed perfectly on the deck of the *Jammy Dodger*.

"Just thought I'd drop in!" said Spike in his rattiest voice to Roddy. Spike walked towards him, wielding the can opener threateningly.

"Do something!" Roddy shouted to Rita.

She only had one option left. She tore open a compartment above her to reveal a big red button. She took a deep breath, closed her eyes, and slammed the button down. There was an immediate reaction as jets fired up underwater and the *Dodger* rocketed forward. Rita held on to the wheel. Roddy tried to dig his claws into the deck to prevent him from sliding towards Spike but it was no use.

"Any last requests?" Spike cackled.

Roddy looked past Spike and at the telephone cord safety harness he was still wearing. It was attached to Whitey's speedboat and it was nearly stretched to its limit.

"Yes," said Roddy, with newfound confidence. "Could you fly, quite suddenly, off the boat, screaming like a girl?"

Spike smiled for a second, until he felt a violent tug and suddenly he was flying backwards off the boat pulled by the telephone cord. He screamed like a girl.

Whitey watched Spike fly past him until the coil was at full stretch once again, and then Spike was flying back towards the speedboat. With an almighty crash, and then a splash, Spike had disappeared right through the floor of the hench-rat's boat, which then started to sink.

TEN

Spike and Whitey made it back to The Toad's lair. They were wet and tired but The Toad had little sympathy.

"You incompetent cheese eaters!" he yelled at them. "You're telling me you had the cable in your grasp and you let them escape?"

The Toad's neck puffed up to the most extreme size and suddenly it burst. Spike fainted in terror.

"It's obvious," The Toad went on, "that I should never have sent rodents to do an amphibian's job." He looked at the clock. "Where is he? Why is he always late?"

A fly buzzed round the clock. The Toad was feeling a bit peckish so he lashed out his tongue, but someone beat him to it. A quicker, stickier, snappier tongue snatched the fly, while The Toad's tongue just stuck to the window.

"Le Frog?" he asked. His eyes swivelled upwards and focussed upon his French cousin dressed in a trenchcoat, sitting on a nearby window.

"Ha, ha, ha . . ." laughed Le Frog from his seat on a nearby pipe. "Bonjour."

"You're late, Le Frog," The Toad said angrily.

"Fashionably late, my lumpy English cousin," said Le Frog. "I know no other way." Le Frog was a mercenary and bounty hunter. He had a strong French accent, but he spoke excellent English.

The Toad went into debrief mode, pacing up and down with his arms behind his back. "Now listen. Rita and her new accomplice have stolen something irreplaceable." He pointed to the plugs where the cable used to be. "A master cable of unique design and purpose. I want it back."

"Is that it?" asked Le Frog, with his hands upturned in a shrug, as if it was the easiest thing in the world. "Don't worry. I'll get it back for you."

"Once it is returned, my plan will be complete. My plan to wash away, once and for all, the curse . . . the scourge . . ." The Toad lowered his voice to a whisper, realising Spike and Whitey could hear him. "*Rats!*"

"Forgive me, my warty English cousin," said Le Frog, "but this bizarre obsession with the rats, it is not good for you. You are becoming . . ." he searched for the correct English expression. "Ah, oui! A mental case."

The Toad tried to contain his anger. "Perhaps you forget that it was a rat who cast me from paradise!"

Le Frog rolled his eyes and pleaded, "Not the scrapbook again!" but it was too late. The Toad had already reached for a large, dusty scrapbook on the shelf.

"My memoirs!" he said, overtaken by melancholy as he flicked through the pages of photographs. "Volume one details the dire and tragic story of my youth."

"Oh, *mon dieu,*" groaned Le Frog. He had heard it all before. The story began in Buckingham Palace. The Toad had been a pet of the young Prince — his most favored pet, in fact — and the prince would take him everywhere. There were photos of The Toad and the Prince frolicking in sunny meadows, boating on the palace lake and sharing a milkshake."

We were inseparable until . . . *it* arrived." The Toad spat out these last two words. The next photo revealed the 'it' to be a pet rat in a golden cage. It was the Prince's birthday present and he looked delighted.

"While the poor boy's head was turned," continued The Toad, "I was taken, torn away from that noble realm, and cruelly plunged into a whirlpool of despair."

"I know, I know . . ." Le Frog said matter-of-factly. "You were flushed away down the loo, right? Boo hoo hoo." He began to mock The Toad. "It is so dark, so cold, so terrible." He was laughing at The Toad.

"You find my pain funny?" asked The Toad.

"I find everyone's pain funny but my own," replied Le Frog. "I'm French."

"Just get the cable!" snarled The Toad, towering over him. He wasn't going to let a frog get the better of him. Le Frog might be a cold-blooded killer, but The Toad wielded the power down in this sewer.

Le Frog snapped his fingers, and several frog mercenaries appeared behind him, ready for action.

"Hench-frogs," announced Le Frog. "We have a mission! We leave immediately!"

"What about dinner?" asked one of the hench-frogs.

Le Frog realized he was right. It was dinnertime. The mission could wait.

"We leave in five hours," said Le Frog. And in true French style, they settled down for a long, leisurely dinner.

ELEVEN

In a quiet sewer, Roddy and Rita were having their own dinner. The moon was streaming through a drain, casting a romantic light onto the *Jammy Dodger*.

"This is quite tasty," said Rita, complimenting the chef.

"Thanks," replied Roddy. "Yes, I don't think it's too bad considering I only had an apple, six raisins, and a box of rice."

He ate another large mouthful as Rita was scraping the last morsel from her bowl.

"That wasn't rice," she said. "It was maggots."

Roddy stopped chewing and swallowed hard. He looked down at his plate. "Well, that explains why it all ran to one side when I put the salt in!"

Unsurprisingly, he suddenly felt full. He patted

the sides of his mouth with his napkin and put down his plate.

"You know," said Rita, wiping her mouth with the back of her hand. "I think we did pretty well today. Maybe I misjudged you a bit. I mean, you're not . . ."

Roddy got up to clear the plates away. "Do I hear an actual compliment coming?"

"Never mind," she said, shaking the thought from her mind.

"No, no, no," pleaded Roddy as he walked over to do the washing up in a cracked tea cup perched on top of a cotton reel. "Say it."

"Well," she began. "You're not entirely the useless, whiney, stuck-up, pompous twit I thought you were."

There was a compliment in there somewhere.

"There," said Roddy. "Was that so hard?

Rita grinned. "Well, we'd better get some rest if we're going to get you home tomorrow." She playfully threw a sleeping bag at Roddy. It was a filthy old sock. Not quite what Roddy was used to, but it would have to do.

As they made up their beds, Rita said, "Tell me about yourself, Roddy."

"Oh, there's not much to tell," he said truthfully.

"You know everything about me," said Rita, "warts and all. I don't even know what you do." It was an ironic thing to say, because of course Roddy had never "done" anything in his whole pampered life.

"I'm in a boy band," he quipped.

"What?" Rita looked confused.

"Yeah, I'm the posh one," he said, making Rita laugh. It felt good to make her laugh, but Roddy didn't want the conversation to continue. It was getting uncomfortable.

"What are your friends like? What's your family like? You do have a family, don't you?" She was being too persistent.

"Oh, brothers, sisters, cousins. Yeah, we're quite a clan," said Roddy, but what started out as sarcasm turned into a big fat lie. "You wouldn't believe the fun we have," he went on, getting caught up in the whole brilliant fantasy, "hanging out at the movies, playing golf, going skiing. And each year on my birthday, we have this huge party. It's just so great!"

"No wonder you want to get home," Rita said.

They both settled down in their sock beds.

"Well . . . I guess tomorrow we'll both get what we want," she said.

They both lay awake, thinking. It had been quite a day and Roddy felt oddly happy.

"Good night," he said, just as he had done the night before in his comfortable Kensington bed. But this time it was a real voice and not an echo that answered him back.

"Good night, Roddy."

Roddy couldn't help but smile.

"Good night," he said again.

Slightly puzzled, Rita said goodnight again.

Roddy enjoyed this so much that he tried it again. "Good night."

"Good night, Roddy," said Rita, emphatically and finally. "Don't let the bedbugs bite."

Roddy smiled and snuggled down, but suddenly he yelped and jumped up again. He had been bitten.

"Seriously," laughed Rita. "Don't let the bedbugs bite."

TWELVE

Roddy was woken on the ship with a start. Rita had pulled the horn on the *Jammy Dodger* to get him up.

"Wakey, wakey!" she said chirpily. "We're getting close to Kensington. Tie down anything loose. It's going to be a bumpy ride."

"Aye, aye, captain," he said, yawning. He couldn't believe he was almost home. He began to tie things down, but knots were not one of Roddy's specialities and he was struggling.

Suddenly a green finger appeared over the side of the boat to help him. It held the string, while Roddy finished the knot.

"Ah, thank you," said Roddy, still half asleep and not realizing exactly what was happening.

It was only when the frog jumped over the side of the boat, ninja-style, that he truly woke up.

"Aargh!" he yelped. Then five more frogs jumped onto the deck.

"Bonjour," they called in unison as they surrounded Roddy.

Rita heard the commotion.

"Hop it!" she yelled to the frogs, but suddenly she came face-to-face with Le Frog who was dangling down from the roof of the wheelhouse.

"Ah, the English little girly. She is so aggressive." Rita and Le Frog were old acquaintances. "I like a woman with a little fire."

He leapt down and took her hand to kiss it. She slapped him across his clammy green face.

"Oh, you're going to pay for that," he threatened. "But first a word from our sponsor . . . Marcel!" Marcel was a frog in a mime costume who hopped into the circle of frogs with a mobile phone strapped to his chest. The phone rang and Marcel flipped it up so it covered his face. The Toad's image appeared on the screen.

"I should have known!" snarled Rita.

"Well done, Le Frog!" The Toad was delighted that Rita and Roddy had been captured. He had been right to send in a fellow amphibian rather than trust those useless rats.

"Now then, Rita. Hand it over," The Toad said.

"Hand what over?" Rita hadn't a clue that she had something that The Toad wanted. The ruby had been smashed into shards of worthless glass. "I don't have it anymore. It was a fake anyway."

"What?" It was The Toad's turn to be confused. "Oh, the ruby!" He dissolved into manic laughter. "Oh, this is rich. The ruby was a pretty thing . . . But nothing compared to the master cable."

Rita was even more puzzled. "The master what?"

"The cable!" said The Toad. "The one you're now wearing as a belt."

Roddy looked at Rita's waist. There was the cable she had used for their getaway. Now she was wearing the cable as a replacement belt to keep her pants up.

Roddy was relieved. "Well, if that's all he wants . . ." but Rita wasn't so eager to give it back. If The Toad had put so much effort into finding it, first with a gang of rats and then a gang of frogs, the cable must be incredibly valuable to him.

"What do you want it for anyway?" she asked.

The Toad was cryptic. "Oh, you'll see. Come the World Cup Final this afternoon!" and he dissolved into manic laughter again, looking every bit the super villain that he craved to be — until he starting choking.

"Okay, okay, cousin," said Le Frog. "Take a breath. Leave it to me. We'll get your cable, kill the rodents and then me and my team can settle down to a decent breakfast."

The frogs began to move in on Rita and Roddy. The mere mention of breakfast had made them extremely hungry, and they wanted to get this over with.

They launched into action. They flip-flopped around the deck, trying to look impressive by striking martial arts poses. It was a ridiculous spectacle, but Rita steeled herself for a fight.

"I've got a plan," whispered Roddy.

She followed his gaze to a fly lying on a spoon on deck having a snooze. Rita was beginning to like Roddy's plans.

Roddy whacked the end of the spoon so the sleepy fly was thrown into the air. "Fly at twelve o'clock!" he shouted.

All the frogs turned. They couldn't help themselves. Their instincts were just too strong. They all lashed out with their tongues to catch the fly at the same moment. Their tongues twisted into a sticky pink knot.

Rita jumped onto the roof of the *Jammy Dodger* and grabbed a tree root that was hanging down through the sewer wall. Tarzan-like, she swung down on the root and hooked on the knot of tongues. Then she let go and crashed back onto deck, while the army of frogs were catapulted off the boat by their tongues. Greed was their undoing.

"No! Get that cable!" shouted Le Frog. He had been the only one who had resisted the temptation of the little fly.

Le Frog lunged for Rita, but she managed to kick him on his back. In that brief moment, Rita realized the *Jammy Dodger* had been dragged into a fierce current.

"Roddy," she called in alarm. "The rapids!"

Roddy whirled round to see a sign:

WATER PURIFICATION — HAZARDOUS

DANGER

HIGH TEMPERATURE

He ran to the wheelhouse and tried to accelerate their way out of the rapids, but the engine cut out. It was no use. The *Jammy Dodger* was going over the waterfall and he could do nothing to stop it.

By now, Le Frog had rebounded and come at Rita once again. While Rita was fighting off Le Frog, she pleaded with Roddy to do something. But what could he do? He looked at the *Jammy Dodger*'s controls, then at the approaching drop, then up at a pipe that spanned across the vast chasm into which the water fell. If only he could get the mechanical arm to grab that pipe . . .

Roddy frantically hit every single button and lever he could see, but the arm didn't move. They were doomed!

The *Jammy Dodger* went over the edge. It hovered for a split second in mid-air while the water dropped down into a massive vertical pipe and disappeared into boiling blackness. Roddy fell backwards screaming. Luckily he fell directly onto the lever that controlled the mechanical arm. The robotic hand shot out and grabbed the pipe, just as the *Jammy Dodger* began to go into freefall. It held fast and the *Jammy Dodger* was now swinging vertically from the pipe. Roddy couldn't hold on and fell head over heels out of the wheelhouse. Luckily, a hand shot out and grabbed him. It was Rita. Her other hand was hanging onto the *Jammy Dodger*.

The two of them were now dangling perilously from the back of the *Jammy Dodger*. They looked at one another. They looked down at the void below them. All of Rita's belongings were falling into the boiling waters below. How on earth were they going to get out of this?

Le Frog flopped down the deck. It was at times like this he was glad to be an amphibian. With his sticky hands and feet, he had no fear of falling. He pulled the cable off Rita's waist and hopped away up the boat. Then he jumped up onto the pipe and sat next to the robotic hand — the only thing stopping Roddy, Rita, and the *Jammy Dodger* from plunging down into the chasm.

"Aha! I have triumphed!" he said victoriously.

"You stupid English, with your Yorkshire puddings and your chips and fish. You thought you could defeat Le Frog?"

He began to count in French as he kicked the first of the three claws off the pipe. Roddy and Rita looked at him with wide-eyed horror.

Le Frog kicked the next claw.

With that Roddy noticed a plastic bundle fall off the boat and he made a wild grab at it, just catching it as Le Frog kicked the final claw off the pipe.

They fell. *The Jammy Dodger* fell.

"Nibble for your life!" yelled Roddy to Rita as they were falling. They both began to nibble at the string holding the plastic bag together and then it unfolded into a gloriously beautiful rat-sized parachute.

A split second later, the *Jammy Dodger* splashed into the hot waters below. A huge spout of steam shot upwards and filled the plastic bag. Suddenly Rita and Roddy were ascending like a hot-air balloon — and fast!

Le Frog didn't know what had happened. One minute he was holding the master cable, revelling in the deliciousness of his victory, and the next his hand was empty!

Le Frog looked up to see Rita waving the cable at him.

"My belt, I think!" she called down to him.

"Goodbye, *Jammy* me old mate," said Rita, as she watched the last part of her beloved boat disappear underwater. But they were still alive and, not only that, they were rising out of the sewers and into the sunshine.

THIRTEEN

Roddy and Rita shot out of the sewer into a beautifully sunny sky. They had made it, thanks to their plastic bag balloon. The whole of Central London was below them, glittering in the sun.

"We're okay, we're okay . . ." Roddy was ranting.

"Try opening your eyes," said Rita.

Roddy opened one eye and yelped. Even with what he'd been through, he still hadn't conquered his fear of heights.

When he'd plucked up the courage to open his eyes again, he took a look at what was below him. "We're over Kensington," he said excitedly.

"Yeah," said Rita in her no-nonsense kind of way. "Only a terrifying nine hundred feet drop between you and a nice comfortable bed." But the hot air in the bag was cooling down and they were descending slowly. They began steering the bag like a paraglider over rooftops.

"Which is your house then?" asked Rita.

Roddy saw some familiar landmarks. *Inverness Gardens ... Vicarage Gate ... Kensington High Street ...* "Try and go left," he said.

So Rita pulled down on her side.

"That's it," Roddy said encouragingly. He was trying to calculate how they could steer over to his street, negotiate all the chimney stacks, and then get just above the chimney of his building. They were losing height all the time.

"This is going to be tricky," he admitted.

Rita glanced at him. "Oh yeah, and everything else has been a piece of cake!"

She had a point.

As they got to his street, he identified each of his neighbour's homes. "Forty-five, forty-seven, forty-nine ..." They were here! "Now!" Roddy yelled.

They both let go of the bag and dropped into the blackness of Roddy's chimney.

FOURTEEN

Roddy and Rita crash-landed on the carpet in Roddy's apartment, spreading soot all over its pristine whiteness. Roddy was finally home.

"Ha, ha! We did it!" He jumped up. "The crew of the *Jammy Dodger* survives!"

Rita took in the elegant surroundings. Roddy may have been home, but her home was lying on a sewer bed below them.

"Oh, oh, oh!" Roddy quickly realised he'd put his foot in it again. "I'm such an idiot. The *Dodger* . . ."

"Wasn't your fault," said Rita. "Quite an adventure though, wasn't it?"

"Rita, I am so sorry," Roddy began, but then inspiration struck, "but I think I might be able to cheer you up."

"Ta-da!" he announced as he opened the jewellery box. "As promised, the Kensington jewels!"

Rita was awestruck. "It's just beautiful."

The ruby sparkled in the sunshine and her face became awash with crimson light.

"And the best part . . ." he gave it a good knock, "unbreakable!"

"I don't know what to say," Rita replied.

"You think it'll be enough?" asked Roddy. "To take care of your family?"

Rita was so choked up, she couldn't speak. She just nodded her head. This was all too much. After everything she'd been through, after all the battling and scavenging to scrape a living, she was being handed the most beautiful, amazing gift. It was the answer to all her prayers.

Roddy then produced another ruby earring. "And maybe this could pay for the *Jammy Dodger Mark II*?" He had thought of everything.

Rita was so overcome with emotion that she just grabbed him and gave him the tightest hug. She didn't seem to want to let go.

Still beaming, Roddy's heart surged with happiness. He had finally proved to her that he was not the blithering, useless twit she first thought he was — and he'd proved it to himself too.

But once again, Rita gave him a reality check. "Well," she said. "I suppose this is it."

Roddy looked at her for a moment, wanting so much for this adventure to continue, wanting so much for her to stay, but all he found himself saying was, "Thank you. For the lift."

"You're welcome," she smiled. Then she turned to go.

She stopped. "Roddy?" she asked. "I don't suppose you'd have time to give me a quick tour."

Roddy felt his heart lift again and he smiled.

"I'd love to meet all your family," Rita added.

"Ah . . ." His smile disappeared.

Roddy couldn't let Rita see that he was just a sad and lonely pet, not after telling her all about his friends and family. The shame and humiliation would be too much. The pretence had to continue.

He held open the door of his electric car for Rita to get in. Then he took her for a spin down what he knew were empty corridors.

"Where is everybody?" he shouted. "Hello! Hell —

ooo! Wouldn't you know it," he laughed. "Just when you need them, all out. Every one of them."

Rita spotted something in the bedroom. "What's that?" she said, pointing to Roddy's cage. It may have been grand, but there was no disguising what it really was.

"Oh, that!" said Roddy, thinking fast. "That's my master bedroom."

"It's a cage," Rita said, pointedly.

Roddy laughed nervously, as if it this was the most ridiculous idea. Needless to say, he failed.

"Will you look at the time . . ." he muttered. He wished he could turn back the clock to the time when he gave her the ruby and she thought the very best of him. "So much to see so little time to see it in," he said as he gestured back to the car. "Shall we?"

Rita stopped him short, and turned him towards her.

"You're all alone up here . . . aren't you?"

Roddy stared back at her, the truth gaping between them. For a moment, it looked as if Roddy was going to confess all, but then the silence was shattered by a bellowing "GOOOAAAALLLLL!" from the next room. Roddy had forgotten all about Sid.

Roddy and Rita looked at one another.

"Who is that?" asked Rita.

SID! Roddy thought. *This could work out very nicely.*

"That . . . would be my brother," said Roddy, and as he said it, the door was booted open and Sid exploded into the room.

"What a game!" he said ecstatically. "I can't believe it!" He began dancing round the room.

"Oh, hello," he said to Roddy. "Where've you been?"

"Rupert," Roddy continued with the introductions, "this is Rita. She's been looking forward to meeting *my brother*." Roddy was desperately hoping that Sid might co-operate with this pretence.

"Obviously," Roddy went on, "there's not a huge family resemblance. I . . . rather got the brains, and . . ." he looked at Sid. "Well, actually I got the looks too, but . . . we're very close. Aren't we, Rupert?"

Sid looked at him open-mouthed. Roddy slowly lifted Sid's bottom jaw with his finger, so his mouth was shut. This wasn't going well.

"Well," Roddy tried to recover the situation. "How time flies when you're having fun." He gestured to Rita. "On with the tour, shall we?" And he tried to lead her away, but Rita didn't move. All she said was, "Hello, Sid."

Roddy's confusion was instant. How could she know his real name? It only took a split second for the truth to sink in. Rita and Sid were both from the sewers. Rita and Sid knew one another!

"Hello, Rita," said Sid. "How's your dad?"

"Better, yeah," replied Rita. "Thanks for asking."

Sid looked at Roddy's face and burst out laughing. "Rupert? What was *that* all about?" He grabbed hold of Roddy in a friendly headlock. "Come here you poor little thing..." He started knuckling Roddy on the top of his head. *This was totally humiliating*, thought Roddy, *and in front of Rita too!*

"Look at his little face. You ever seen anything so pathetic?" Sid thought it was hysterical. "*Brothers?* Ha! All Mr. Lonely has got is a couple of dolls and a little wheel to run round in this cage." And with that, Sid walked off, still laughing. "What a loo-hoo-hoo-ser!"

Rita watched Sid until he disappeared back into the living room. Then she turned to Roddy.

"It's okay," she said softly. She tried to take Roddy's hand, but he pulled it away.

Roddy didn't want her pity. "It's okay?" he snapped. "Look at this place, Rita. Look at my home. It's a palace." She lived in the sewers, after all, on a boat made from junk! "I can do whatever I want, whenever I want. I'd say that was a little more than okay. What do I need *friends* for? What do I need *family* for? I'm sorry," he said, raising his chin to try to regain some of his lost pride, "but if you've got everything you need, I really have to get going. I've got a serious infestation to deal with."

Rita knew Roddy was embarrassed but there was nothing she could do to repair the situation.

"I'll . . . say goodbye then, Roddy St. James. Of Kensington." It was the only thing she could think of to say. And she walked off towards the bathroom.

Roddy wanted to stop her. There was so much he wanted to say, but instead he just watched her go. He thought she would never respect him, knowing that he had lied, knowing that he was a pet. He looked around. The dolls sat grinning at him as usual. His luxurious cage was sitting in the corner. He had everything a rat could want — just no one to share it with.

Then he heard the toilet flush. Rita was on her way home.

Sid was surprised to see Roddy marching into the living room. He looked different — not quite so pathetic.

"Come on England!" Sid said to the television. England was winning the World Cup Final against Germany. "This is fantastic!" Sid said to Roddy. "Come 'ere, bro! Rupert's missing his Roddsy Woddsy." He still thought the situation was hilarious. "You crack me up, mate, you really do. 'Ere' have a cheese puff."

Roddy took the cheese puff and crushed it into Sid's hand. "Move over," he snarled.

Sid was surprised, but he didn't move.

"MOVE OVER!" Roddy ordered and then he plonked himself down beside Sid. He grabbed Sid's can and took a big sip of his drink. It was all Sid's fault. *All of it!* He had spoiled everything.

"Roddy," said Sid. "Word of advice, mate. Take it easy with the drink. Seriously, or you'll never make it till half time."

The words hit Roddy like a thunderbolt. "What did you say?"

"The bathroom," explained Sid. "I'm waiting till half time. I don't want to miss any of the game."

Suddenly all the pieces of The Toad's plan fell into place — why The Toad had been so desperate to get back that master cable. The Toad had said, "You'll see. Come the World Cup Final." And this was the final. Soon everyone in the up-top world would be going to the toilet — *at the same time!*

"The whole city will be flushed away," he said urgently to Sid. "Come with me." And he began to pull Sid off the sofa.

"But what about the game?" asked Sid. Clearly, he had difficulty deciding which was more impor-tant — the World Cup Final or saving his species from being wiped out by an evil amphibian.

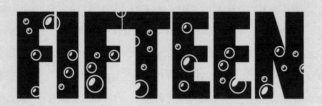

FIFTEEN

Down in the sewers, the whole population was out in the square watching a huge TV screen. World Cup fever had hit the sewers just as much as it had hit the up-top world above. Rita's mum and dad were there with the children. Everyone was excited and enjoying the game.

Watching the crowd from above was The Toad.

"Enjoy your last moments, vermin," he said with satisfaction, but his moment of reflection was interrupted as Spike and Whitey came in dragging Rita with them. They had captured her as she entered the sewers from Kensington.

"Ah, Rita," said The Toad. "It's so good of you to return the cable."

Le Frog appeared and snatched the master cable from around Rita's waist.

"At last," said The Toad triumphantly. "It's mine." He held it up and laughed manically. As he laughed, he slammed the cable into its socket and with a dramatic gesture he said, "Let there be light!"

The motors began to run and giant cogs groaned to life. There was a shower of rust and then, with a deafening grinding sound, the sewer floodgates slowly began to open for the first time in decades. This was going to completely expose this small city to the main sewer.

Up in Roddy's apartment, Sid and Roddy were standing on the toilet seat again, just as they had done before.

Sid was mock-pleading with Roddy, "Please don't flush me, Roddy. I can't survive down there. I've gone soft."

Roddy slapped him. "I want *you* to flush *me*," said Roddy. "I'm going back."

Sid looked at him in disbelief.

"Rita's in terrible danger. Everyone's in terrible danger. Now you like it here don't you?" he asked

"Oh, yes!" said Sid. "I like it here very much."

"Will you be good to Tabitha, the little girl who looks after me?"

Sid liked the sound of this. He liked the sound of

this a lot. "I'll be good as gold to her, Roddy. I will be the *best pet EVER*."

The irony of what Sid was saying wasn't lost on Roddy. Sid had laughed at Roddy for being a pet and now he was eager to swap!

"The place is all yours," said Roddy. "Right, let's get those bubbles going. I've got a big job to do down there."

Roddy dived into the toilet bowl. Sid pulled the handle and, once again, flushed him away.

"So long, Sid!" called Roddy as he swirled in the whirlpool of water.

"So long Rodnick St. Something of Someplace or other," said Sid, before rushing back to catch the end of the first half.

Down in the sewers, the same rat that had spoken of the great flood was on his soap box again. He was telling anyone who would listen of his great prophecy.

"And lo!" he announced. "A chosen one shall come from above and he shall be our saviour from the great flood."

At that very moment he was flattened by Roddy who fell from a pipe above him. *Could this be the savior?*

"I'm terribly sorry," said Roddy, helping the rat up, before dashing off to find Rita. Meanwhile a TV presenter was announcing the World Cup score. England was winning two–zero with only twenty minutes to go before the end of the first half. He didn't have long to find Rita or to save all the rats that lived in the sewers.

Then he noticed the huge floodgates slowly opening, and dangling from a pipe in front of them was Rita!

Roddy had to do something . . . and fast. He frantically looked around him. There were a cluster of stalls selling random things to the crowd — newspapers, umbrellas, rubber-glove balloons, and fans. *Perfect!* he thought.

Within minutes, Roddy was floating up to Rita in a little flying machine made from an inflated rubber glove and a fan. Rita was amazed and relieved to see him.

"Rita, I'm so sorry," he shouted. "I've been such a fool. You were right about me. You were right about everything. I should just have admitted it but I was afraid you wouldn't like me anymore —"

"Do you think we can talk about this after you've rescued me?" Rita said cutting him off.

Roddy untied her quickly, just as The Toad and his hench-rats began to come up to the pipe in an elevator.

Roddy told Rita of The Toad's grand plan to flush away all the rats, but she already knew. The Toad had taken great delight in telling her that he was going to wipe out her entire family, along with all the other sewer rats.

"We've got to warn everyone!" said Roddy as they began to float away.

"Stop them!" shouted The Toad. At his order, one of his hench-rats leapt towards them, without realising he was perched perilously on a pipe. He plummeted into the water below. Frustrated, The Toad picked up a staple gun and began firing it at the rubber-glove balloon. A staple pierced through it and suddenly the whole balloon burst.

"Oh dear," said Roddy as they fell — *smash, bang* — into The Toad's lair.

Spike, Whitey, and Thimblenose were waiting for them.

The Toad pushed his way forward and confronted Roddy and Rita.

"So you thought you could make a fool of The Toad, eh?" As he said this, the remains of Roddy's rubber-glove balloon floated down and landed on The Toad's head.

"You don't need us for that," quipped Rita.

"Oh, you think you're *sooo* clever, don't you?" he said, brushing off the balloon. "Well, I'll be the one laughing when every last revolting rat is flushed away, for I shall repopulate the sewer with . . . THESE!" He laughed hartily and pulled back a curtain to reveal millions of tadpoles. He looked admiringly at all his babies.

"Ew," said Roddy and Rita in disgust.

"We need to get downstairs and pull out that cable!" whispered Roddy to Rita.

"How?" she asked. "It's impossible."

"England is winning," Roddy said. "Anything's possible."

He had come up with an escape plan before and he felt confident he could do it again. He looked around him and noticed some pipes running under his feet. His eyes followed them to their source — they led to the liquid nitrogen tanks The Toad had tried to freeze them with earlier. He reached down and yanked up the small pipe. Immediately liquid nitrogen began to pour out. Roddy found it difficult to control as it began to snake all over the place. He threw it at Thimblenose and Ladykiller who were instantly frozen solid. Ice began to form on the floor and spray all over the hench-rats freezing them all in bizarre positions.

Roddy grabbed Rita's hand and they ran.

The Toad fired his tongue out towards Rita while Spike made a grab for Roddy. They both missed and The Toad ended up ensnaring Spike instead. He threw Spike carelessly over his shoulder so Spike landed, bottom first, in the jar of tadpoles.

"Arrghh, Whitey," he yelped. "They're biting me. Help!"

Whitey tried to run over, but he was stuck in the ice. The Toad slipped on the ice and careened into Spike. Rita and Roddy ran to the elevator and pressed the button. They could escape! But they got a nasty surprise. When the elevator doors opened, Le Frog and his hench-frogs were inside.

"Hello, my little ratty friends," said Le Frog. "Seize them!"

The hench-frogs chased Roddy and Rita away from elevator. This time Rita grabbed the liquid nitrogen pipe and swiped it over the floor sending out a sheet of ice. The frogs were frozen instantly in an elaborate ice sculpture.

The Toad saw how the others were failing and began to approach.

"Do I have to do everything myself!" he screamed in frustration.

Rita lifted the pipe to freeze him too, but there was no liquid nitrogen left. The tanks were empty. Rita dropped the pipe and ran with Roddy, followed in hot pursuit by The Toad.

SIXTEEN

The Toad leaped onto the rickety old pipe and blocked Roddy's and Rita's escape. The pipe was hissing and leaking gas under the weight of the fat Toad, but he didn't notice. The whistle had just been blown to signal the end of the first half of the match. The Toad's plan was about to reach its glorious conclusion and nothing was going to stop him now.

"You're too late to do anything," he gloated. "You and your kind are finished."

"Oh yeah?" Rita said defiantly. "Well come and get us then you warty windbag."

The Toad wasn't going to let a rat talk to him like that. He growled and took a step forward, his foot landing heavily on a weakened pipe joint. Liquid nitrogen began to seep out and it shot up his leg, freezing his foot to the pipe.

Then they heard the first toilet flush, followed by many more. Suddenly, hundreds of slugs poured out of the main sewer below screaming. The flood must be on its way.

"The gate," shouted Roddy to Rita. It was the only hope they had to save the city. "Back this way! Come on!" They both headed back towards the roof of The Toad's lair but Rita was suddenly hauled backwards. The Toad had grabbed her with his long sticky tongue and now he was preparing to do the same to Roddy.

"If I'm going, you're both coming with me," he yelled, and fired his tongue out towards Roddy.

"Just go Roddy!" Rita pleaded, but he wasn't going to leave her behind.

Roddy dodged the next attack. The Toad retracted his tongue and prepared to fire again. Roddy quickly looked around. In an instant, he knew exactly what to do. He leaped up and grabbed hold of a smaller pipe.

The Toad's tongue lashed out again. Roddy dodged and The Toad's tongue got caught in the gear mechanism of the floodgates. As the gears turned, it pulled The Toad's tongue further and further in. He was caught and there was no way he could get his tongue free.

Roddy could now see the huge tidal wave racing down the main sewer. In seconds the wave would hit the city and all the innocent rats, including Rita's family, would be engulfed in water.

The Toad's tongue was at full stretch and because his foot was still attached to the liquid nitrogen pipe, The Toad and the pipe were being drawn into the gears.

Roddy leapt down from his pipe to try to save Rita, who was still in The Toad's clutches.

In his rage The Toad called for Le Frog.

Le Frog rolled his eyes, casually put down his magazine, straightened his collar and leapt into action. He jumped in front of Roddy, cutting off the path to Rita.

"Let's finish this," Le Frog challenged.

Roddy looked across at The Toad and Rita. The Toad glared at Roddy. Then, quite suddenly, The Toad threw Rita off the pipe. She was falling like a stone.

Roddy grabbed Le Frog and squeezed him like a rubber toy. Le Frog's tongue involuntarily shot out and connected with the same pipe The Toad was frozen to. It stuck fast. Still holding on to Le Frog, Roddy leapt, Tarzan-style, off his pipe. He swung through the air towards Rita and just grabbed her in time. Under their weight, the nitrogen pipe ruptured a little.

Roddy and Rita swung through the air and landed safely on the rooftop of The Toad's lair, just in time to see the wave rushing towards The Toad. As the wave hit The Toad, the freezing nitrogen pipe ripped apart.

Down below, Rita's dad saw the wave coming. "Wave! Wave!" he yelled, but all the football fans were so caught up with World Cup fever that they misunderstood and waved their hands from one side of the crowd to the other.

"No!" yelled Rita's dad. "GIANT wave!"

The crowd all turned to see the huge tidal wave bearing down on them. Everybody screamed.

Roddy and Rita were up on the rooftop watching.

"Please work," Roddy muttered, crossing his fingers. The final part of his plan was in place. It just *had* to work. And *NOW!*

Suddenly, the liquid nitrogen pipe fell into the water. Instantly, the water began to freeze, spreading through the rushing wave.

Just as the crest of the wave was about to engulf the crowd, it froze in mid-air. Great long icicles hung over the crowd who were all holding their breath.

There was a moment of stunned silence . . . and then the crowd began to cheer.

"Look, it's Roddy and Rita!" shouted Rita's mum, pointing up at the roof.

"So it is. Good on ya, girl!" called up her dad.

"Hooray for Millicent Bystander!" said a voice in the crowd below, and they all began chanting, "Millicent! Millicent!" Roddy was a hero! He couldn't quite believe it, that all these rats were calling his name — sort of. He suddenly felt connected to this underground community and that was a new and amazing feeling for Roddy. He finally felt part of something.

"Roddy," said Rita. "You're a hero!"

Both Roddy and Rita looked down to see that Le Frog was still in Roddy's clutches. Roddy had been so tense, he hadn't let go. As soon as he did, Le Frog was yanked away by his over-stretched tongue. He collided with The Toad, whose tongue was still entangled in the gears.

"You wretched vermin," The Toad yelled to Roddy and Rita. "I'll make you pay for this."

"Oh give it a rest, cousin," said Le Frog, seeing the reality of the situation. There was no way either of them was in a position to be issuing threats. They were beaten and he knew it.

Roddy and Rita laughed together. They really had done it!

Roddy turned to Rita, suddenly looking very serious.

"Rita," he began. She looked him in the eyes as he continued, "Life down here with you has meant more to me than anything Up Top ever has. So, I was wondering... if you do build a *Jammy Dodger Mark II...*" Roddy paused, "You wouldn't happen to need a first mate, would you?"

Rita smiled at Roddy knowingly, and extended her hand. Roddy did the same. They both spit into their hands and shook on it. There was no need for words.

"Okay!" Roddy called to Rita as he put the finishing touches a nameplate: THE JAMMY DODGER II.

Rita smiled at Roddy's handiwork and pressed a button on the *Jammy*'s dash. A brand new mechanical arm lifted Roddy up and placed him on the *Jammy*'s deck with Rita's family who were there to celebrate the christening of the *Jammy Dodger II*. A crowd of rats cheered and waved from the dock. Even Spike and Whitey were there.

Roddy smiled mischievously at Rita. "Shall we?" he asked.

Roddy pointed at a button marked TURBO.

Rita smiled and said, "Go for it."

In an instant, massive hydrofoil boosters thrashed around in the water and with a *BOOM*, the boat sped off. The partygoers all clapped and hollered as the *Jammy Dodger II* took off at full speed.

As they headed for uncharted waters, Rita turned to Roddy and playfully asked, "Where are we going?"

Roddy smiled and shrugged. "I don't know. But we're gonna get there very fast!"